Hot Wheels™

Thrill Ride

By Ace Landers
Illustrated by Dave W

SCHOLASTIC INC.
New York Toronto London Auckland
Sydney Mexico City New Delhi Hong Kong

ISBN 978-0-545-28444-8

12 11 10 9 8 7 6 5 4 3 2 1 11 12 13 14 15/0

Printed in the U.S.A. 40
First printing, February 2011

Today is a big day at the track.

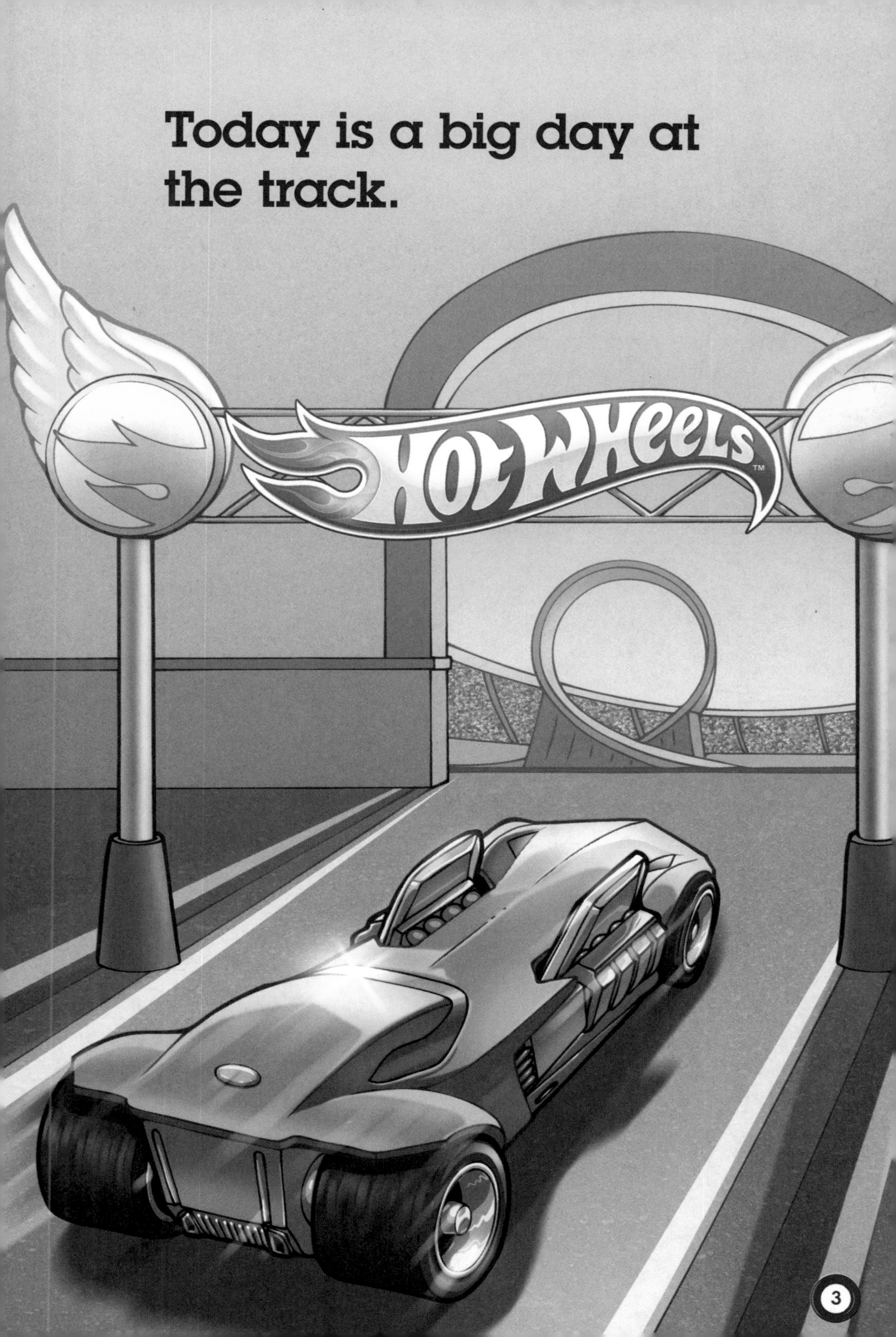

Cars and motorcycles will do awesome stunts!

The drivers are ready.

The fans are ready.

The race begins.

The first stunt is ahead.

The orange car is first on the ramp.

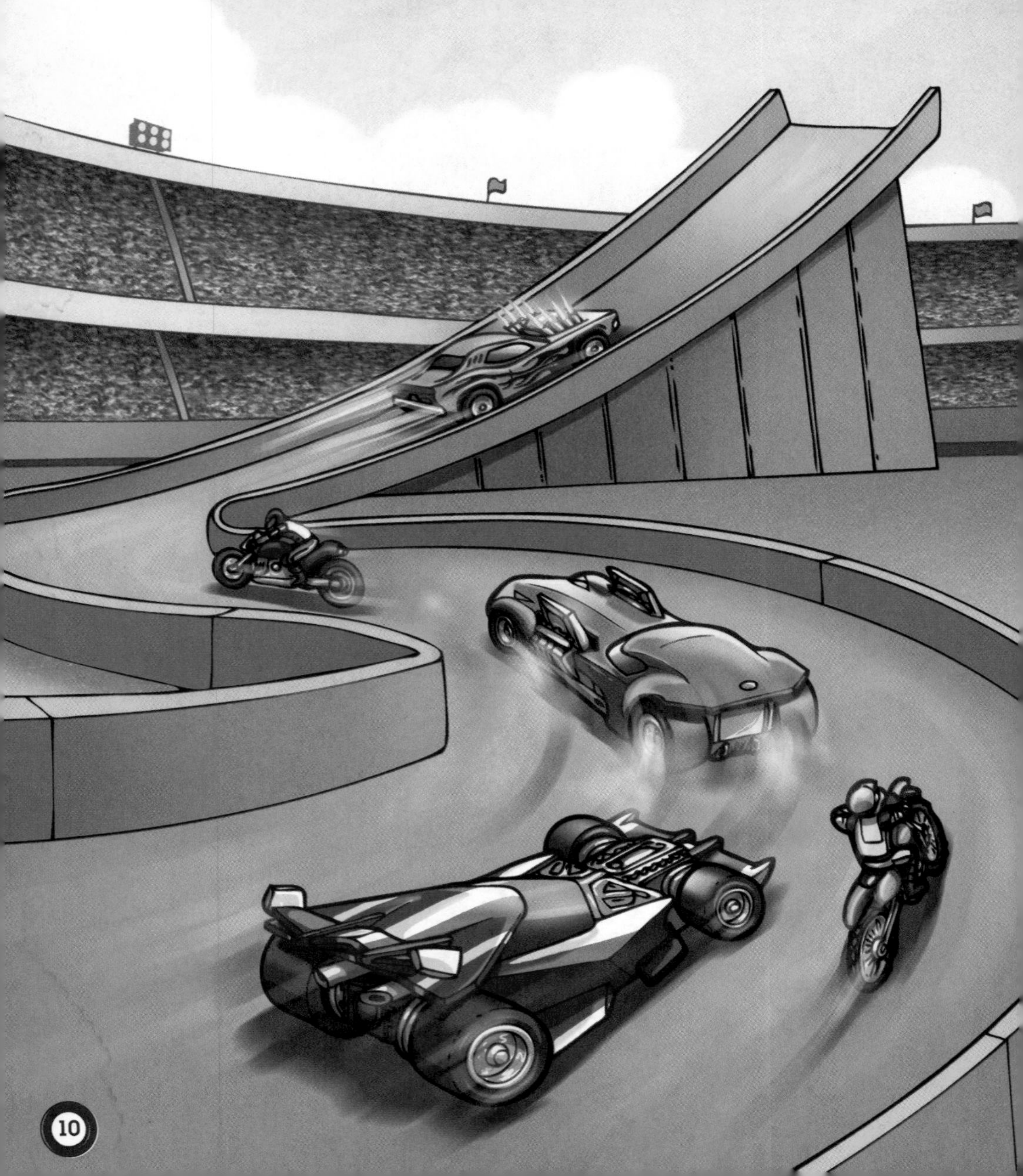

It jumps through the fire!

The motorcycles are close behind.

These bikes have power!

Everyone lands!

The racers drive to the next stunt.

This track has sharp turns.

The cars and bikes zoom around the turns.

One racer loses control and hits the wall.

The other racers dodge the crash!

There is another ramp.

Everyone must jump over a lake!

The cars fly through the air.

The motorcycles flip!

The racers did it!

There is one last stunt.

It is a giant loop.

The racers drive as fast as they can.

Will they make it all the way around the loop?

The racers speed around the loop!

That was a thrill ride!